This edition first published in Great Britain in
1995 by Macdonald Young Books

Photoset in 16/24 Meridien

Printed and bound in Belgium by Proost N.V.

Macdonald Young Books
Campus 400
Maylands Avenue
Hemel Hempstead HP2 7EZ

British Library Cataloguing in Publications Data
available

ISBN 0 7500 1705 8
ISBN 0 7500 1706 6 (pb)

Jeanne Willis

The Princess and
the Parlour Maid

Illustrated by Pauline Hazelwood

MACDONALD YOUNG BOOKS

Buckingham Palace

1
The Mayflower

Out in the cobbled street, Hannah joined hands with Martha to make an arch. The other girls danced under it, holding each other's skirts and singing, "Thread the tailor's needle, Thread the tailor's needle, The tailor's blind and he can't see, So thread the tailor's needle!"

A young woman stood on the steps watching, with a baby in her arms. "Come on," she smiled, "it's past bedtime."

"Oh!" protested Hannah, "but I'm not a bit tired, Mamma."

"Don't you want a story?"

Hannah waved goodbye to her friends. Soon, she was sitting in front of the mirror, having her hair brushed.

"What colour was the princess's hair?" she asked.

"A pretty, dark blonde," replied her mother," she wore it in ringlets. I'm afraid mine spent most of its time stuffed under a cap! All the maids at the palace had to wear a uniform. Black stockings, a gown and a neck handkerchief, pinned cornerwise behind."

"Tell me the bit about when you first met the princess," begged Hannah. Her mother shook her head, but Hannah looked so disappointed, she pulled up a stool, smoothed her skirts around her and began:

"When I was only ten, I left Derbyshire to work as a kitchen maid at Kensington Palace for the Duchess of Kent."

"What was she like, the Duchess of Kent?" asked Hannah.

"I hardly knew her," said her mother, "servants weren't allowed to talk to their mistresses. I do know that she was German…and that she had lost two husbands. Princess Drina's father died when she was only eight months old."

"Princess Victoria, you mean," corrected Hannah.

"Everybody called her Drina then," said her mother. "Her first name was really Alexandrina. Her grandmamma called her 'The Mayflower' because she was born in May...now put your nightdress on and get into bed, dear."

Hannah sulked. "No pouting!" scolded her mother, "you're lucky to have a bed to yourself. I had to share a freezing attic with Emma and Dora, the scullery maids."

"I remember that first night, climbing the back stairs in my stockinged feet so as not to wake the others. It was pitch black, apart from my candle flickering in the draught. I was about halfway up when I almost fell over a tiny girl, sitting in the shadows."

"I know who she was!" said Hannah, excitedly.

2
Little Miss Lonely

"'Hello,' said an inquisitive voice, 'who are you, pray?'

'I'm Lilly, Miss,' I said. I could tell she wasn't a servant by the way she spoke.

'I'm Drina, and I should like you to talk to me.'

What she was doing up at that late hour, I don't know.

'Oh, I'm not allowed to talk to the likes of you, Miss,' I said, 'I'm only a maid.'

'Then I command you to!' said the Princess, playfully. She had a doll on her lap, most beautifully dressed. She told me it was her best friend."

"Didn't she have brothers or sisters?" asked Hannah.

"There was Charlie, her stepbrother, but he lived in Germany, and her stepsister, Fedore, was much older than her."

"What about her governess?" asked Hannah.

"Louise Lehzen was her governess. Drina adored her, but they'd had a row that day…Lehzen insisted on pinning a sprig of holly under Drina's chin to remind her to hold her head up like a queen."

"Did she know she was going to be Queen one day?"

"No, darling, not then. Her 'Uncle King' was still on the throne. She said he was fat and wore greasy make-up to hide his wrinkles. We giggled so much, we had to stuff our fists in our mouths in case the Butler heard us.

I told the Princess I'd better go, saying I had to be up at five to blacklead the range.

'What's blackleading the range?' she wanted to know, 'it sounds fun! I've got to do horrid algebra and deportment. I'd much rather go for a ride on Dicky the Donkey. Uncle York gave him to me.'

She asked me to meet her in secret after tea, and we'd drive to the chestnut trees and back."

"Did you go?" asked Hannah, innocently.

Her mother shook her head, "I was on my knees with exhaustion. The Housekeeper had me scrubbing floors until my knuckles bled. She had a fondness for gin and could be cruel. We used to call her 'Pug'."

"Poor Mamma!" said Hannah, "weren't you jealous of all Drina's lovely things?"

"No," said her mother, "We were poor, but we were never lonely. The Princess would have swopped all the silver spoons in the palace for a true friend." Just then, the baby started to cry and her mother went to comfort him.

"You will come back and tell me the rest, won't you?" pleaded Hannah.

3
I Will be Good

Hannah's baby brother was asleep now.

"Did you ever speak to Princess Drina again, Mamma?" asked Hannah.

Her mother put down the petticoat she was folding. "Not until I was almost grown-up and a parlour maid," she replied, "but there was always gossip below stairs, like the scandal about a Mr. Conroy being the Duchess's lover."

"Was it true?" Hannah wanted to know.

Mamma frowned, "It's not nice to talk about those things, dear, so we won't."

"Oh," said Hannah, pulling a face.

"Don't be a puss or I shan't tell you what happened next," teased her mother.

"Oh, plea...se."

"Very well! There I was, black to my elbows from making up the fire," said her mother, "when I saw Princess Drina curled up, small as you please behind a cushion…sobbing into her pet spaniel's fur.

I tried to tiptoe past, but the scuttle caught on the sill and the princess looked up at me, her big blue eyes red with weeping. 'Oh, Lilly!' she sobbed. I asked if I should fetch the doctor, but she said she hated doctors and that wasn't the problem. I didn't know whether to curtsy or run."

"What was the matter with her?" asked Hannah.

"It seems Lehzen had left a history book lying around 'accidentally on purpose' which showed who was next in line for the throne, and there was Drina's name, almost at the top! She peered at me over the cushion and whispered, 'Lilly, I am to be Queen!'"

"I should love to be Queen," said Hannah, "why ever was she crying?"

"It all came as a bit of a shock," said her mother, "she was very young, you know. Up until then we'd only ever had funny, old kings…mad as hatters, mostly. Anyway, she soon dried her eyes.

'I told them I will be good,' she said. 'Do you think I will make a good Queen, Lilly?'

'I know it, Miss,' I said, 'Lord knows the monarchy couldn't be worse!'"

"You never said that!" squealed Hannah.

"Oh, but I did!" said her mother, "I suddenly found my tongue and forgot my station. Luckily, she laughed. She wasn't a bit stuck-up. 'I'll have to go, Lilly, or that beetle, Conroy, will send out a search party...come along, Dash!'

Then she picked up the little lumps of coal I'd dropped, put them back in the scuttle and ran down the corridor.

'Lilly!' boomed a voice. It was Pug. I was for it!"

4
Through the Keyhole

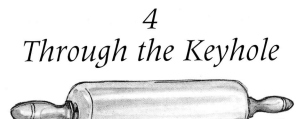

"Did you get into awful trouble for talking to the Princess?" Hannah wanted to know.

Her mother shuddered. "I was hauled into the kitchens and when Pug heard what I'd done, she went for me with a rolling pin. She'd have killed me if Pappa hadn't pulled her off."

"You weren't married to Pappa then, were you?"

"No, Pappa was the Under-Butler. I thought him handsome but I never expected him to give me a second look. I was just a common parlour maid."

"You're not a bit common, Mamma," insisted Hannah, "and I think Pug was a monster."

Her mother smiled, "Pug was more to be pitied than scolded," she said, "the house was at sixes and sevens because we were always understaffed...never more so than just before the Princess's eighteenth birthday. Poor Pug nearly had the vapours trying to get everything organised."

"I bet Drina had a lovely party," sighed Hannah.

"Wonderful!" exclaimed her mother, "the whole country celebrated! She'd grown into such a lovely girl. Even Pug cheered up and let us share some wine and cake and Pappa asked me to dance. He was the only one I ever told about my friendship with Drina."

"Didn't you even tell Emma and Dora?"

"They would never have believed me!" said her mother. "Did I ever tell you about the note I sent to her?"

"No."

"Pappa could write beautifully," she continued, "and when old King William died…"

"I thought the King was called George!" interrupted Hannah.

"No, dear. Poor old George died when Drina was eleven…his brother William became King and he died just after her eighteenth."

"Was she very sad, Mamma?"

"Of course…and it meant she would
be Queen even sooner than she thought.
That's why I sent a note, to say I was
thinking of her. Pappa nearly got caught
sneaking it in."

Hannah gasped. "How?"

"Well, the Princess slept in the same room as her mother and never got up before seven, but that day, the Duchess woke at six. The Archbishop and Lord Conyngham wanted to talk to Drina in the sitting room. The whole palace was buzzing."

"Why, what was happening?" asked Hannah.

"I'll tell you in a minute," said her mother, "Pappa watched the whole thing through the keyhole."

5

Goodbye, Drina

Hannah's mother took a sip of water.

"So, there was Drina in her nightdress with the Lord and the Bishop..." urged Hannah, "then what, Mamma?"

"Then Lord Conyngham said, 'The King expired at twelve minutes past two this morning, ma'am. You are Queen!'"

"What did Drina do, mamma? I should have burst into tears."

"Oh, she was **Victoria** now, dear. Not Drina…'Drina' was gone forever. She didn't cry. She stood up straight…like this…and held her hand for him to kiss. Pappa said she looked every inch a Queen, tiny as she was."

"Did she still have to do as her mamma told her?"

"No," laughed her mother, "the very first thing she did was insist on having her own bedroom."

It was getting late. Hannah's mother stood up and drew the curtains.

"What about when she got her crown…you can't leave that bit out!" cried Hannah. "Tell me how she was woken up by the cannons in Hyde Park and about the…"

"Very quickly then…or Pappa will be home and I shan't have supper ready."

Her mother's eyes looked dreamy. "It was June the 28th," she remembered, "the cannons went off at four in the morning to announce the coronation. Emma and Dora and I…we were so excited!

We'd persuaded Pug to let us have the morning off to watch the procession going to Westminster Abbey. You should have seen the coaches, Hannah! Pulled by gleaming cream horses…people from all walks of life crowding onto the street to see them go by."

"Did you see them put the crown on her head at the Abbey?" asked Hannah.

"No darling…remember I was only a servant. The Abbey was full of grand people…the Duchess, Kings and Queens from foreign lands, Lords, Ladies…Lord Melbourne was there, bless him. He was more like a nice, old pappa than a Prime Minister. I believe Lehzen was there."

"But did you see Victoria in her white gown with the gold lace?"

"Yes! Suddenly, Emma started jumping up and down and pointing to one of the carriages. 'It's her little majesty!' she cried, quite overcome with emotion.

'She's beautiful,' I agreed.

'Aye, but not as beautiful as you, Miss Lilly,' said a young man standing behind me. Can you guess who he was, Hannah?"

"Not Pappa!"

"I should say!" winked her mother.

Just then, they heard his key in the lock.

6
A Gift from the Palace

Hannah shut her eyes and pretended to be asleep, but just as her mother tried to make a hasty retreat, she grabbed hold of her skirt.

"Mamma, did you miss Victoria when she went to live at Buckingham Palace?"

"Of course, but hush, now...Pappa's home."

"But did you ever hear from her again?"

Her mother looked thoughtful.

"Yes," she replied. "Not long after I married Pappa, Victoria fell deeply in love with her cousin, Albert. They got married, as you know, and about a year later, their first child was born."

"The Princess Victoria?"

"That's right. Anyway, I took the liberty of sending Queen Victoria a card of congratulations and told her that I had a baby daughter too."

"Me," said Hannah.

Her mother nodded. "Well, as you can imagine, I never expected a reply...not from the Palace! I doubted the Queen would even remember who I was. Then a week later, a parcel arrived. Inside was the sweetest letter and something all done up in tissue paper printed with the royal crown."

"What was it, Mamma?"

"Something for you."

"What...a bonnet? A gown?"

"No...remember the little toy Drina was playing with the first time I bumped into her in the dark?"

"Yes," said Hannah, "the one Lehzen made dresses for?"

"Well, there she is!" said Mamma, pointing to the doll Hannah had been holding throughout the story.

"What…Milly?" exclaimed Hannah, scarcely able to believe it, "My Milly?"

"Yes…she was given to you by Queen Victoria. Milly was her favourite doll too, you know. Or so she said."

As Hannah drifted happily off to sleep, she dreamt about a palace far away. And in the palace there was a young Queen with pretty, dark blonde hair putting her own little girl to bed, and the little girl was saying, 'Mamma, please tell me a story.'

And the Queen began:

'Once upon a time, I was sitting with my favourite doll on the back stairs to the attic when I met a little maid called Lilly…'